S0-DZC-305

Who Has Horns?

written by Pam Holden

We see horns
on the cow.

We see horns on the sheep.

We see horns
on the lizard.

7

We see horns
on the rhino.

9

We see horns on the buffalo.

We see horns
on the giraffe.

We see horns on the goat.

We see horns
on the dinosaur.